Copyright © 2012, 2013 by Lemniscaat, Rotterdam, The Netherlands
First published in The Netherlands under the title *Gewoon gek*
Text & illustration copyright © 2012 by Ingrid and Dieter Schubert
English translation copyright © 2012 by Lemniscaat USA LLC • New York
All rights reserved.

No part of this book may be reproduced or utilized in any form or by any means, electronic or
mechanical, including photocopying, recording, or any information storage and retrieval
system, without permission in writing from the publisher.

First published in the United States and Canada in 2013 by Lemniscaat USA LLC • New York
Distributed in the United States by Lemniscaat USA LLC • New York

Library of Congress Cataloging-in-Publication Data is available.
ISBN 13: 978-1-935954-26-2 (Hardcover)
Printing and binding: Worzalla, Stevens Point, WI USA
First U.S. edition

Ingrid &
Dieter Schubert

Opposites

LEMNISCAAT

Up

Down

Big

Small

Wet

Dry

Hide

Seek

Cold

Hot

Brave

Scared

Naughty

Nice

Alone

Together

Happy

Sad

Normal

Crazy

Fight

Make up

Asleep

Awake

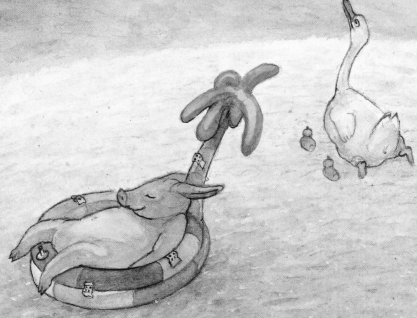